中英雙書

神奇魔指

羅爾德・達爾 *Roald Dahl* ◎文
昆丁・布雷克 *Quentin Blake* ◎圖
顏銘新◎譯

The Magic Finger

振聲高中
張湘君 校長 強力推薦

開啟孩子創造力
由閱讀羅爾德 · 達爾開始

◎張湘君（振聲高中校長）

　　羅爾德 · 達爾（1916-1990）是一位備受矚目的英國兒童文學大師級人物。他的十九部作品，部部想像力驚人，書中創意點子令人拍案叫絕，受到廣大小讀者的喜愛，甚至還有個羅爾德 · 達爾日（9月13日），當天全球粉絲們紛紛舉辦各種活動，向羅爾德 · 達爾這位偉大的作者致敬。

　　我個人是達爾迷，他的作品不管是各種版本的作品、錄音帶或錄影帶甚至考題，我都廣泛蒐集。在國立臺北教育大學兒童英語教育研究所及亞洲大學應用外語學系教授「英美兒童文學」期間，更是將達爾的作品列入學生修課必讀書單，也不時在課堂中播放其作品改拍的電影《飛天巨桃歷險記》、《巧克力工廠的祕密》、《吹夢巨人》、《小魔女》及《女巫》，以增加學生對達爾作品不同面向的探索及體悟。

達爾創作之兒童讀物所以受人矚目，除了寫作手法高明外，主要是因為其大量運用獨特的「殘酷式幽默」，令學校老師不安，孩子的家長不悅，評論家不屑。達爾常在作品中敘述種種殘忍的場面或手段，例如把人斬成肉泥、絞成肉醬、搗爛他、砸碎他等等，這些事看在小孩子的眼裡，是有趣、誇張、惹人捧腹大笑，然而看在大人眼裡，盡是血腥恐怖、殘忍不堪，一文不值。

　　例如，《神奇魔指》書中描述一個小女孩的指頭有神奇的魔力，當她氣憤、失去控制的時候，全身會先變得很熱、很熱，右手的指尖也會開始產生帶著奔馳閃光的電流，而這電流會跳出去觸擊令她氣憤的人，他們的身上就會接二連三的發生怪事。達爾運用了「殘酷式幽默」來傳達孩子愛護動物的心聲，誇張、有趣、三不五時帶點殘忍場面的情節，非常能吸引小讀者閱讀。

達爾有四個孩子，每天晚上他在孩子睡覺前，也都會說故事給他們聽，因此，他的魅力不只是在文字，擅長用聲音來說故事應該也算是他的另一項特異功能。達爾常自己造字，來增加口說故事時的生動。以《大大大大的鱷魚》為例，書中有許多英文動詞鮮活傳神，如 squish、squizzle、swizzle、swoosh、Trunky 等一般字典裡查不到的「達爾專用字」，讀者可仔細推敲這些字的來源，或輕鬆略過，但不要忘了享受其中的音韻樂趣。尤其對白鮮活有趣的英文章節，可鼓勵小讀者從事英語話劇或讀者劇場的演出。

　　達爾是個喜歡搞怪的人，他搞怪的能力無遠弗屆，尤其擅長創造魔法的情節和運用幻想的元素，這可能跟達爾的母親在他和他的姊妹們孩提時代，常常說巨人等虛構人物的北歐神話故事有關。然而達爾對自己的作品要求嚴格，絕不重複使用相同的點子，往往一年才能醞釀出一個滿意的故事。

　　總之，達爾是那種只想要給孩子快樂的作家，他的作品中，孩子是絕對的王，孩子的對手（通常是大人）通常都會得到嚴厲不留情的懲罰。這些過程驚悚的反大人作品，如同《小鬼當家》一系列的電影，披露小孩其實擁有遇事沉著、冷靜、聰明、機智應對的大能力，著實讓大人驚訝！而小讀者閱讀達爾作品後，應該也能學到不管遇到多大困難，都要鎮定自若，勇敢面對，更要積極的想辦法，用自己的智慧和經驗去戰勝它！

紅花要有綠葉襯，三本書的插畫皆由昆丁・布萊克執筆，相得益彰。昆丁・布萊克是當代英國兒童文學界最負盛名的插畫家和作家，得過英國兒童讀物的各項大獎，他風格滑稽特異的插畫與達爾的精闢文字可謂天生一對，是無可取代的組合。

近年來，世界上有為的政府莫不以打造創造力國度為施政主軸，希望國家百姓能具備自我創造的意識，勇於創新、冒險與超越，以開闊的思維和自在的態度展現獨特、新奇和有趣之個人色彩，並從不斷嘗試創造的過程中發現學習樂趣。

達爾作品總能帶給讀者豐富的想像力、創造力及閱讀的樂趣，在此我誠摯的、歡喜的將它的新版推薦給臺灣的大小讀者。

神奇魔指

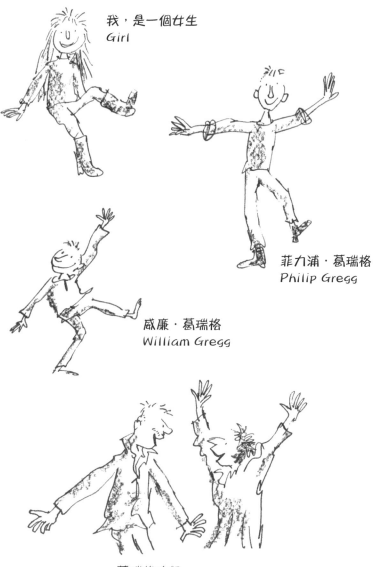

人物介紹

我，是一個女生
Girl

菲力浦・葛瑞格
Philip Gregg

威廉・葛瑞格
William Gregg

葛瑞格夫婦
Mr and Mrs Gregg

我家隔壁的農場是葛瑞格先生和葛瑞格太太家的。葛瑞格家有兩個小孩，兩個都是男生。他們的名字是菲力浦和威廉。有時候我會去他們的農場和他們一起玩。

　　我是女生，我八歲。

　　菲力浦也是八歲。

　　威廉比我們大三歲，他十歲。

　　什麼？

　　噢，好吧！那……

　　他是十一歲。

　　上個星期，葛瑞格家發生了一件非常好玩的事情。我將盡我所能的把它全都告訴你們。

最近，葛瑞格先生和他的兩個兒子最愛做的事情就是打獵。每到星期六早上，他們就會帶著獵槍，前往森林去尋找動物或鳥類來射擊。連菲力浦都有自己的獵槍──他才八歲而已呢！

　　我無法忍受打獵行為！就是**無法忍受**！對我來說，男人和男孩子們純粹只是為了樂在其中就去獵殺動物，這是非常沒有道理的。因此每一次我越過農場去找他們，總試著勸菲力浦和威廉別再去了，可是他們只會嘲笑我。

甚至有一次，我在勸葛瑞格先生的時候，他直接從我身邊走過去，根本就當我是隱形人。

　　後來，某個星期六早晨，我看見菲力浦和威廉跟著他們的爸爸從森林裡走了出來，還扛著一隻可愛的小鹿。

　　實在讓我覺得很抓狂，所以我對著他們扯開嗓門大聲吼叫。

那兩個男孩不僅嘲笑我，還做鬼臉給我看。葛瑞格先生甚至要我回家去，並且警告我，要我注意自己的禮貌。

哼！那就別怪我這麼做了！

我火大了！

就在我還來得及控制自己之前，我做了一件我從沒有想過要做的事——

我把神奇魔指對準他們所有的人！

噢，天啊！天啊！我甚至對根本不在場的葛瑞格太太也施了魔法——我把魔法施給了葛瑞格全家人！

幾個月以前，自從我的老師——冬冬老小姐出事之後，我就一直不斷的告訴自己，再也不要把神奇魔指對準任何人了！

　　可憐的冬冬老小姐。

　　那一天我們都在教室裡，當時她正在教我們拼字。「站起來……」她叫我：「把『貓』的英文拼出來。」

　　「那還不簡單……」我說：「K— a— t。」

　　「妳這個笨女孩！」冬冬小姐說。

　　「我不是笨女孩！」我大聲反駁：「我是很棒的小女孩！」

　　「妳給我去牆角那邊罰站。」冬冬小姐說。

接著我開始抓狂、火冒三丈，然後把我的神奇魔指非常用力的指向冬冬老小姐……

　　你猜猜看，發生了什麼事？

　　她的臉上幾乎立刻開始長出**鬍鬚**，又長又黑的鬍鬚，就像是長在貓咪臉上的鬍鬚，只不過更長，而且長得好快！在我們都還來不及反應時，鬍鬚就已經長到她的耳朵後頭了。

　　當然囉！我們全班開始哄堂大笑。冬冬小姐便說：「你們，所有的人，誰願意告訴我，你們究竟看到什麼瘋狂好笑的事情呢？」

　　等到她轉過身，在黑板上寫字的時候，我們又發現，她竟然還長出了一條**尾巴**！好大一條毛茸茸的大尾巴！

我沒辦法告訴你們，後來她發生什麼事情；如果你們好奇，想知道冬冬老小姐現在是不是已經恢復正常了，答案是——沒有，而且永遠也不會。

　　神奇魔指是我與生俱來的超能力。

　　我很難告訴你們，究竟我是怎麼操縱這個能力的，因為連我自己也不是很清楚！

　　不過每次在我很生氣、很生氣，氣到爆的時候，就會發生⋯⋯

　　全身會變得很熱、很熱⋯⋯

　　熱到右手的指尖開始產生極度可怕的刺痛感⋯⋯

剎那間，一道閃光從我身上發射出去，就像帶著電流奔馳的光束……

那道光從指尖跳出去觸擊那個讓我抓狂的人……

在那之後，神奇魔指便開始讓那些人身上發生一些怪事……

現在神奇魔指的魔力就降臨在葛瑞格全家人身上，而且想要收也收不回來了。

我跑回家去，靜待怪事發生。

事情發生得太突然了。

現在就讓我來告訴你們，到底發生了什麼事？因為在所有事情結束後的隔天早上，我便從菲力浦和威廉那兒聽到了完整的故事過程。

　　就在我把神奇魔指指向葛瑞格全家的當天下午，葛瑞格先生和菲力浦、威廉又再次去打獵。這一次他們想打野鴨，所以朝湖邊去。

　　第一個鐘頭裡，他們打到了十隻鳥兒。

　　接下來的一個鐘頭裡，他們又打到了六隻。

「今天運氣真是不錯！」葛瑞格先生大呼：「這是目前為止打得最好的一次了！」瞧他一副洋洋得意的樣子。

　　就在那時，四隻野鴨飛過他們的頭頂。牠們飛得很低，低到很容易就會被打到。

　　砰！砰！砰！砰！連續四槍。

野鴨飛走了。

「竟然沒打到！」葛瑞格先生說：「真可笑。」

然而，出乎意料的是，四隻野鴨卻回轉身來，朝著槍口直直飛了過來。

「嘿！」葛瑞格先生說：「這些鴨子到底是在搞什麼？這次可是牠們自個兒找的！」於是又朝牠們開了槍，兩個男孩也跟著開槍。但是又一次，全部都沒打中！

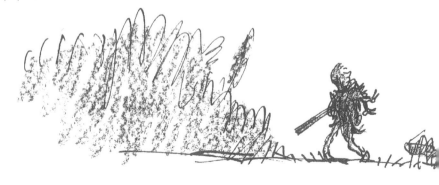

葛瑞格先生的臉都羞紅了。「都是因為光線的關係，」他說：「天色太暗，看不清楚了。我們回家吧。」

於是他們帶著先前打到的十六隻鳥兒準備回家。

可是那四隻鴨子卻不肯放過他們父子三人，他們要離開的時候，鴨子開始在他們三人頭頂上拍翅盤旋著⋯⋯

葛瑞格先生可不喜歡這樣。「走開！」他大叫，接著又朝鴨子開了很多槍，但是都沒打中。他根本打不到！回家的路上，那四隻鴨子不斷在他們頭頂上空盤旋著，根本趕不走。

那天晚上，等菲力浦和威廉都上床之後，葛瑞格先生想到外面拿一些木柴生火。他穿過庭院時，突然間，聽到空中有一隻野鴨子在叫。

他停下腳步，抬頭看了看。夜晚很安詳，淡黃色月兒掛在山坡的樹梢頂端，天空中布滿了點點星光。接著，葛瑞格先生聽到一陣振翅低飛過頭上的嘈雜聲，

然後在夜空中看到四隻鴨子的身影，一隻隻靠攏著繞著屋子附近飛行。

　　葛瑞格先生忘了柴火，快步跑進屋裡。現在他感到相當害怕，也不喜歡剛剛看到的那些景象。不過他沒有向葛瑞格太太提起，只說：「來吧！我們睡吧，我累了。」

於是他們就上床睡覺了。

第二天早晨時，葛瑞格先生第一個醒來。

他張開眼睛。

正想伸出手，把手錶拿來看看時間。

但是，手呢？

「這可有趣了，」他說：「我的手到哪兒去了？」

他靜靜的躺著，想著到底是怎麼回事。

也許那隻手不知道什麼時候弄傷了吧？

他嘗試用另一隻手。

但另一隻手也沒了！

他坐起來。

有生以來，他第一次看到自己看起來像什麼東西！

他大吼一聲，跳下床來。

葛瑞格太太也醒了，睜開眼後，看到葛瑞格先生站在地板那兒，她也大叫一聲。

因為葛瑞格先生現在成了一個只有小小一丁點的人！

他也許有一把椅子座位的高度，但是絕對不會超過。

而且就在他手臂原來的地方，竟然長出一對鴨翅膀！

「喔……喔……天哪……」葛瑞格太太臉色發紫，大叫說：「親愛的，你怎麼了？」

「妳應該是說，**我們**怎麼了吧！」葛瑞格先生大聲叫嚷著。

這一次換葛瑞格太太跳下床，跑去看看鏡子裡的自己。可是她不夠高，看不到鏡子。而且她甚至比葛瑞格先生還矮，她也是手臂不見了，卻長出一對翅膀。

「哦！哦！哦！哦！」葛瑞格太太啜泣著。

「這一定是巫婆幹的好事！」葛瑞格先生驚叫。接著他們兩個開始拍動翅膀，在房裡跑了起來。

　　一分鐘後，菲力浦和威廉衝進來。同樣的情況也發生在他們身上──有翅膀，卻沒了手臂。而且他們**真的**很小，就像知更鳥那麼一點大。

　　「媽媽！媽媽！媽媽！」菲力浦啾啾叫著：「妳看，媽媽，我們會飛耶！」然後他們就飛向空中。

　　「立刻給我下來！」葛瑞格太太說：「你們飛太高了！」下一句話還沒說出口，菲力浦和威廉已經直直往窗外飛出去了。

葛瑞格先生和葛瑞格太太跑到窗邊向外看出去。兩個小不點般的男孩，現在已經高高在天空中了。

接著葛瑞格太太就對葛瑞格先生說：「親愛的，你認為我們也能飛那麼高嗎？」

「我看不出來有什麼不行？」葛瑞格先生說：「來吧！我們試試看！」

葛瑞格先生開始用力拍著他的翅膀，突然之間，就向上飛起來了。

葛瑞格太太也跟著做同樣的動作。

「救命啊！」她開始向上飛時，一邊大叫著：「救救我！」

「來吧，」葛瑞格先生說：「別害怕。」

因此他們飛出了窗戶，高高的飛入天空，沒多久，他們就追上了菲力浦和威廉。

　　很快的，他們全家人就在一塊兒飛了一圈又一圈。

　　「噢，這不是太美妙了嗎！」威廉大聲喊叫：「我一直想知道當一隻小鳥是什麼感覺！」

　　「妳的翅膀會不會太累啊？親愛的？」葛瑞格先生問葛瑞格太太。

　　「一點也不會，」葛瑞格太太說：「我可以一直

飛！」

　「嘿，看看下面那兒！」菲力浦說：「有人闖入我們的花園！」

　他們往下一看，就在他們的下方，在他們的花園裡，有四隻**巨大**的野鴨！那些鴨子跟人類一樣大，而且更離譜的是，牠們長出像人類一樣長的手臂，卻沒有翅膀！

只見四隻野鴨排成一列，擺動著手臂，鴨嘴巴抬得高高的，正要走進葛瑞格家的房子。

「等一下！」小小的葛瑞格先生大叫，往鴨子們的頭頂飛下來，大喊：「走開！那是我的房子！」

鴨子們抬頭瞧了一眼，呱呱叫著。帶頭的那隻鴨子伸出手打開房門，走了進去，其他鴨子跟在後面，然後門就關上了。

葛瑞格一家人飛了下來，停在靠近門的牆上。葛瑞格太太開始哭泣。

　　「哦，親愛的！哦，親愛的！」她泣訴著：「牠們把我們的房子占據了。怎麼辦？無處可去了！」

　　現在連孩子們也低聲哭了起來。

　　「夜裡我們會被貓或狐狸吃掉！」菲力浦說。

　　「我想睡在自己的床上！」威廉說。

　　「好了，」葛瑞格先生說：「光哭是沒有用的，幫不了什麼忙。我來告訴你們，現在應該怎麼做。」

　　「怎麼做？」他們問。

　　葛瑞格先生看著他們，微笑說：「我們要來做一個鳥巢。」

　　「鳥巢？」他們說：「我們有辦法嗎？」

　　「我們**必須**完成它，」葛瑞格先生說：「我們總得有個地方睡覺。跟我來！」

　　他們飛到一棵高樹上，就在樹頂上，葛瑞格先生挑了一個築巢的地方。

　　「現在我們需要樹枝，」他說：「很多很多的小樹枝。去吧，你們全部都去，找到樹枝後，帶回來這裡。」

　　「可是我們沒有手啊！」菲力浦說。

「那麼就用你們的嘴巴吧。」

葛瑞格太太和孩子們飛走了。不一會兒，他們嘴裡叼了樹枝回來。葛瑞格先生接過樹枝開始築巢。

「要再多一點，」他說：「我還要更多、更多、更多的樹枝。繼續找。」

鳥巢逐漸成形。葛瑞格先生很熟練的把樹枝編織在一起。

過了一段時間之後，他說：「樹枝已經夠了，現在我需要的是樹葉、羽毛或是類似的東西，好讓巢裡頭柔軟又舒服。」

築巢的工作持續進行著。花了好長一段時間，最終於完成了。

　　「試試看！」葛瑞格先生說著，便向後跳了一步。他對於自己的作品相當滿意。

　　「噢，好棒哦！」葛瑞格太太喊叫道，走了進去並且坐下來：「我覺得，我好像隨時可以生出個蛋來！」

　　其他人也都走進巢中，靠在她身旁。

　　「這裡好暖和！」威廉說。

　　「而且住得這麼高，真的好有趣，」菲力浦說：「我們也許很嬌小，可是在這麼高的地方，沒有人可以傷害我們。」

　　「可是食物怎麼辦？」葛瑞格太太說：「我們一整天都沒有吃到東西了。」

「說的也是，」葛瑞格先生說：「那麼我們飛回屋子去。趁那些鴨子沒看到的時候，我們從沒關著的窗戶進去拿罐餅乾。」

　　「噢！可是我們會被那些髒兮兮的大野鴨啄成碎屑！」葛瑞格太太驚叫。

　　「我們會很小心的，親愛的！」葛瑞格先生說完之後，全家人就往房子飛去了。

　　可是當他們飛到房子那邊的時候，發現所有的門窗都關上了，沒空隙可以進去。

　　「你瞧瞧！那隻野蠻的鴨子在我的火爐上煮東西！」葛瑞格太太飛過廚房的窗戶時大聲叫著：「真是太過分了！」

「還有你看！那隻還握著我心愛的獵槍！」葛瑞格先生大吼。

「其中一隻躺在我的床上！」威廉從天窗望進去時大喊。

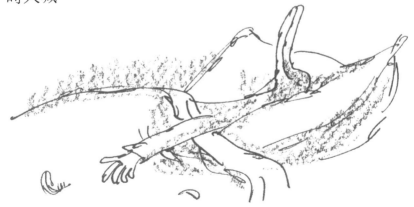

「還有一隻在玩我的電動火車！」菲力浦大聲嚷著。

「噢，親愛的！噢，親愛的！」葛瑞格太太說：「這些鴨子已經占據了整間房子了！房子再也拿不回來了。那我們要吃什麼東西啊？」

「我寧願去死也不要吃蟲子。」菲力浦說。

「我也不要吃蛞蝓。」威廉說。

葛瑞格太太把他們倆拉了過來，懷抱在她的翅膀下。「不要擔心，」她說：「我會把蟲子和蛞蝓剁得很碎，你們根本不會發覺有什麼不對——好吃的蚯蚓漢堡和可口的昆蟲漢堡。」

「噢，不要！」威廉大喊。

「絕不！」菲力浦說。

「好噁心！」葛瑞格先生說：「不能因為我們長了翅膀，我們就得吃鳥吃的東西。我們可以吃蘋果啊！我們的樹上滿滿都是啊。來吧！」

於是他們飛到蘋果樹上。

可是如果不能好好的拿在手裡，吃蘋果可沒那麼容易。每一次只要試著咬下去，蘋果就會被牙齒給推開。後來，他們每個人只能吃到幾小口而已。漸漸天開始變黑了，他們全都飛回窩裡，乖乖躺下睡覺。

就在那個時候，我回到家裡，拿起電話想打給菲力浦，想知道他們全家是不是還好。

「喂？」我說。

「呱！」另一頭有一個聲音回應。

「你是誰？」我問。

「呱──呱！」

「菲力浦，」我說：「是你嗎？」

「呱──呱──呱──呱──呱！」

「噢，閉嘴！」我說。

然後就傳來一陣很可笑的聲音，聽起來好像是有

隻鳥在笑。

　　我急忙把電話給掛斷了。

　　「噢，神奇魔指！」我叫道：「你對我的朋友幹了什麼好事？」

那天晚上，在樹上高高的鳥巢裡，葛瑞格先生和太太還有菲力浦和威廉快要入睡了，一陣大風吹起。那棵樹從一邊晃到另外一邊，每個人都害怕鳥巢會掉

下去，葛瑞格先生也一樣害怕。接著雨來了，雨下了又下，雨水灌進巢裡，每個人全身溼透了——噢，那真是一個很糟糕、很糟糕的夜晚！

清晨，伴隨著溫暖的太陽終於來臨了。

葛瑞格太太說：「謝謝老天爺，總算過去了！我再也不要在鳥巢裡睡覺了！」她站起身來，朝旁邊看過去……

「救命啊！」她大聲尖叫：「看！看下面那裡！」

「是什麼東西啊？我親愛的。」葛瑞格先生邊問邊站了起來，並且向另一邊瞄過去。

他這輩子從沒有那麼驚嚇過！

樹下站了那四隻像人一樣高大的野鴨，其中三隻手上拿著他們的槍。一隻拿著葛瑞格先生的，一隻拿著菲力浦的，一隻則拿著威廉的。

所有槍口都直挺挺的向上瞄準鳥巢。

　　「不！不！不要！」葛瑞格先生和太太一齊大聲叫了出來：「不要開槍！求求你們不要開槍！」

　　「為什麼不？」其中一隻鴨子說。是那隻沒有拿槍的鴨子開口：「你們總是對著我們開槍。」

　　「噢，可是那是不一樣的！」葛瑞格先生說：「我們得到獵鴨的**許可**。」

　　「是誰准許的？」鴨子問。

　　「我們彼此准許的。」葛瑞格先生說。

「很好，」鴨子說：「那麼現在**我們**將彼此允許可以射擊你們。」

（我真想看看那個時候葛瑞格先生的神情。）

「噢，**求求你！**」葛瑞格太太哀求：「我的兩個小孩和我們都在上面，你們不可以射我的小孩！」

「但昨天你們射死了**我的**小孩，」那隻鴨子說：「你們把我的六個小孩全部都射死了。」

「我再也不會了！」葛瑞格先生

大叫：「永遠，永遠，永遠！」

「你說的是真的嗎？」鴨子問。

「**真的！**」葛瑞格先生說：「只要我還活著，我永遠不會再射殺任何一隻鴨子！」

「那可不行！」鴨子說：「還有鹿怎麼辦？」

「只要你們願意把槍放下，無論你說什麼，我都會照做！」葛瑞格先生大叫：「我再也不會射另一隻鴨子或鹿，或是任何動物！」

「你能對我信守承諾嗎？」鴨子說。

「我會！我會！」葛瑞格先生說。

「你會把槍給扔掉嗎？」鴨子問。

「我會砸個粉碎！」葛瑞格先生說：「以後你們再也用不著擔心我或是我的家人獵殺動物了。」

「好極了，」鴨子說：「現在你們可以下來了。

還有，我想稱讚你蓋的鳥巢。第一次就能築成這樣，
非常難得。」

　　葛瑞格先生和太太，還有菲力浦、威廉，跳出鳥
巢飛了下來。

接著他們眼前一團黑，什麼也看不到。瞬間他們

經歷了一種奇妙的感覺，然後耳朵聽見一陣大風吹著。

接著在他們眼前的一片黑變成藍色、綠色、紅色、

金色。突然間他們四個人就站在可愛燦爛的陽光下，

在自己的花園裡，在房子旁邊。而且，全部恢復正常
了。

「翅膀不見了！」葛瑞格先生驚呼：「我們的手臂回來了！」

「我們不再是小不點了！」葛瑞格太太笑著說：「噢，太高興了！」

菲力浦和威廉都快樂得跳起舞來。

然後，就在他們頭上高高的
天空裡，傳來一陣野鴨子的
叫聲，抬頭往上一看，只見那
四隻鳥兒在蔚藍的天空下
顯得靈巧可愛，
緊靠在一起朝森
林裡的湖飛去。

　　大約半小時

之後，我走進了葛瑞格先生的花園裡。我很想看看事
情到底怎麼了。我承認，我很期待最壞的狀況發生。
我在門口停了下來，向裡面盯著看，好一幅古怪的景
象啊──

角落裡，只見葛瑞格先生正在用大榔頭將三把獵槍砸成小碎片。

另一個角落，葛瑞格太太正把漂亮美麗的花朵放在十六座小土堆上。後來我才知道那是前一天被射死的野鴨的墳墓。

菲力浦和威廉站在花園中間，身旁放著一袋上好的麥子。他們被許多鴨子、野白鴿、麻雀、知更鳥、雲雀，還有各種我不認得的鳥兒包圍著，而鳥兒們正在享用兩位男孩一把一把撒落的麥子呢！

「早安，葛瑞格先生！」我說。

葛瑞格先生放下他的榔頭盯著我看。「我的名字不再叫作葛瑞格了，」他說：「為了紀念那些有羽毛的朋友們，我已經把我的姓從葛瑞格改成愛蛋了。」

「而我是愛蛋太太。」葛瑞格太太說。

「發生了什麼事情？」我問道。他們四個好像全部都變得怪裡怪氣的。

於是，菲力浦和威廉就開始告訴我整件事情的來龍去脈。他們說完之後，威廉說：「妳看！鳥巢就在那裡！有看到嗎？就在那棵樹梢上！那就是我們昨天過夜的地方！」

　　「**全都是**我自己築成的，」愛蛋先生驕傲的說：「每一根樹枝都是。」

　　「如果妳不相信我們，」愛蛋太太說：「就進屋子裡去看浴室一眼，裡面真是一團糟！」

　　「牠們把浴缸的水盛得很滿，」菲力浦說：「牠們一定是整個晚上都在裡面游來游去！到處都是羽毛！」

　　「鴨子喜歡水啊，」愛蛋先生說：「真高興牠們有段愉快的時光。」

正好那個時候，從湖邊某處傳來了一聲很響亮的「砰」！

「有人開槍了！」我大聲叫。

「那應該是吉姆庫柏，」愛個蛋先生說：「他和他那三個兒子。這麼瘋狂的開著槍，看樣子應該是庫柏他們一家人。」

突然間，我整個火冒了起來⋯⋯

接著全身發燙⋯⋯

我的指尖開始產生極度可怕的刺痛感。我感覺得到，在我的身體裡面有一股能量不斷、不斷的累積起來……

　　我轉身用最快的速度衝向湖邊。「嘿！」愛蛋先生大喊：「怎麼了？妳要去哪裡？」

　　「去找庫柏！」我喊了回去。

　　「怎麼了？」

　　「你們等著瞧！」我說：「今天晚上他們會在樹上築巢過夜，他們每一個人都會！」

ROALD DAHL
The Magic Finger

The farm next to ours is owned by Mr and Mrs Gregg. The Greggs have two children, both of them are boys. Their names are Philip and William. Sometimes I go over to their farm to play with them.

I am a girl and I am eight years old.

Philip is also eight years old.

William is three years older. He is ten.

What?

Oh, all right, then.

He is eleven.

Last week, something very funny happened to the Gregg family. I am going to tell you about it as best I can.

Now the one thing that Mr Gregg and his two boys loved to do more than anything else was to go hunting. Every Saturday morning they would take their guns and go off[1] into the woods to look for animals and birds to shoot. Even Philip, who was only eight years old, had a gun of his own.

I can't stand hunting. I just can't *stand* it. It doesn't seem right to me that men and boys should kill animals just for the fun they get out of it. So I used to try to stop Philip and William

from doing it. Every time I went over to their farm I would do my

best to talk them out of it, but they only laughed at me.

I even said something about it once to Mr Gregg, but he just walked on past me as if I weren't there.

Then, one Saturday morning, I saw Philip and William coming out of the woods with their father, and they were carrying a lovely young deer.

This made me so cross that I started shouting at them.

The boys laughed and made faces at me, and Mr Gregg told me to go home and mind my own P's and Q's[2].

Well, that did it!

I saw red[3].

And before I was able to stop myself, I did something I never meant to do.

I PUT THE MAGIC FINGER ON THEM ALL!

Oh, dear![4] Oh, dear! I even put it on Mrs Gregg, who wasn't there. I put it on the whole Gregg family.

For months I had been telling myself that I would never put the Magic Finger upon anyone again——Not after what happened to my teacher, old Mrs Winter.

Poor old Mrs Winter.

One day we were in class, and she was teaching us spelling. "Stand up," she said to me, "and spell cat."

"That's an easy one," I said. "K —a —t."

"You are a stupid little girl!" Mrs Winter said.

"I am not a stupid little girl!" I cried. "I am a very nice little girl!"

"Go and stand in the corner," Mrs Winter said.

Then I got cross, and I saw red, and I put the Magic Finger on Mrs Winter good and strong[5], and almost at once . . .

Guess what?

Whiskers began growing out of her face! They were long black whiskers, just like the ones you see on a cat, only much bigger. And how fast they grew! Before we had time to think, they were out to her ears!

Of course the whole class started screaming with laughter, and then Mrs Winter said, "Will you be so kind as to tell me what you find so madly funny, all of you?"

And when she turned around to write something on
the blackboard, we saw that she had grown a *tail* as well!
It was a huge bushy tail!

I cannot begin to tell you what happened after that, but if any of you are wondering whether Mrs Winter is quite all right again now, the answer is *NO*. And she never will be.

The Magic Finger is something I have been able to do all my life.

I can't tell you just *how* I do it, because I don't even know myself.

But it always happens when I get cross, when I see red . . .

Then I get very, very hot all over . . .

Then the tip of the forefinger of my right hand begins to tingle[6] most terribly . . .

And suddenly a sort of flash comes out of me, a quick flash, like something electric.

It jumps out and touches the person who has made me cross . . .

And after that the Magic Finger is upon him or her, and things begin to happen . . .

Well, the Magic Finger was now upon the whole of the Gregg family, and there was no taking it off again.

I ran home and waited for things to happen.

They happened fast.

I shall now tell you what those things were. I got the whole story from Philip and William the next morning, after it was all over.

In the afternoon of the very same day that I put the Magic Finger on the Gregg family, Mr Gregg and Philip and William went out hunting once again. This time they were going after wild ducks, so they headed towards the lake.

In the first hour they got ten birds.

In the next hour they got another six.

"What a day!" cried Mr Gregg. "This is the best yet!"

He was beside himself[7] with joy.

Just then four more wild ducks flew over their heads.

They were flying very low. They were easy to hit.

BANG! BANG! BANG! BANG! Went the guns.

The ducks flew on. "We missed!" said Mr Gregg. "That's funny." Then, to everyone's surprise, the four ducks turned around and came flying right back to the guns.

"Hey!" said Mr Gregg. "What on earth are they doing? They are really asking for it this time!" He shot at them again. So did the boys. And again they all missed!

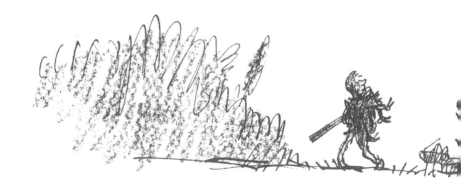

Mr Gregg got very red in the face. "It's the light," he said. "It's getting too dark to see. Let's go home."

So they started for home, carrying with them the sixteen birds they had shot before.

But the four ducks would not leave them alone. They now began flying around and around the hunters as they walked away.

Mr Gregg did not like it one bit. "Be off!" he cried, and he shot at them many more times, but it was no good. He simply could not hit them.

All the way home those four ducks flew around in the sky above their heads, and nothing would make them go away.

Late that night, after Philip and William had gone to bed, Mr Gregg went outside to get some wood for the fire.

He was crossing the yard when all at once he heard the call of a wild duck in the sky.

He stopped and looked up. The night was very still. There was a thin yellow moon over the trees on the hill,

and the sky was filled with stars. Then Mr Gregg heard the noise of wings flying low over his head, and he saw the four ducks, dark against the night sky, flying very close together. They were going around and around the house.

Mr Gregg forgot about the firewood, and hurried back indoors. He was now quite afraid. He did not like what was going on. But he said nothing about it to Mrs Gregg. All he said was, "Come on, let's go to bed. I feel tired."

So they went to bed and to sleep.

When morning came, Mr Gregg was the first to wake up.

He opened his eyes.

He was about to put out a hand for his watch, to see the time.

But his hand wouldn't come out.

"That's funny," he said. "Where is my hand?" He lay still, wondering what was up.

Maybe he had hurt that hand in some way?

He tried the other hand.

That wouldn't come out either.

He sat up.

Then, for the first time, he saw what he looked like!

He gave a yell and jumped out of bed.

Mrs Gregg woke up. And when she saw Mr Gregg standing there on the floor, she gave a yell, too.

For he was now a tiny little man!

He was maybe as tall as the seat of a chair, but no taller.

And where his arms had been, he had a pair of duck's wings instead!

"But[8] . . . but . . . but . . . " cried Mrs Gregg, going purple in the face, "My dear man, what's happened to you?"

"What's happened to both of us, you mean!" shouted Mr Gregg.

It was Mrs Gregg's turn now to jump out of bed.

She ran to look at herself in the glass. But she was not tall enough to see into it. She was even smaller than Mr Gregg, and she, too, had got wings instead of arms.

"Oh! Oh! Oh! Oh!" sobbed Mrs Gregg.

"This is witches' work!" cried Mr Gregg. And both of them started running around the room, flapping their wings.

A minute later Philip and William burst in. The same thing had happened to them. They had wings and no arms. And they were *really* tiny. They were about as big as robins.

"Mama! Mama! Mama!" chirruped Philip. "Look, Mama, we can fly!" And they flew up into the air.

"Come down at once!" said Mrs Gregg. "You're much too high!" But before she could say another word, Philip and William had flown right out the window.

Mr and Mrs Gregg ran to the window and looked out. The two tiny boys were now high up in the sky.

Then Mrs Gregg said to Mr Gregg, "Do you think we could do that, my dear?"

"I don't see why not," Mr Gregg said. "Come on, let's try."

Mr Gregg began to flap his wings hard, and all at once, up he went.

Then Mrs Gregg did the same.

"Help!" she cried as she started going up. "Save me!"

"Come on," said Mr Gregg. "Don't be afraid."

So out the window they flew, far up into the sky, and it did not take them long to catch up with Philip and William.

Soon the whole family was flying around and around together.

"Oh, isn't it lovely!" cried William. "I've always wanted to know what it feels like to be a bird!"

"Your wings are not getting tired, are they, dear?" Mr Gregg asked Mrs Gregg.

"Not at all," Mrs Gregg said. "I could go on for ever!"

"Hey, look down there!" said Philip. "Somebody is walking in our garden!"

They all looked down, and there below them, in their own garden, they saw four *enormous* wild ducks! The ducks were as big as men, and what is more, they had great long arms, like men, instead of wings.

The ducks were walking in a line to the door of the Greggs' house, swinging their arms and holding their beaks high in the air.

"Stop!" called the tiny Mr Gregg, flying down low over their heads. "Go away! That's my house!"

The ducks looked up and quacked. The first one put out a hand and opened the door of the house and went in. The others went in after him. The door shut.

The Greggs flew down and sat on the wall near the door. Mrs Gregg began to cry.

"Oh, dear! Oh, dear!" she sobbed. "They have taken our house. What shall we do? We have no place to go!"

Even the boys began to cry a bit now.

"We will be eaten by the cats and foxes in the night!" said Philip. "I want to sleep in my own bed!" said William. "Now then[9]," said Mr Gregg. "It isn't any good[10] crying. That won't help us. Shall I tell you what we are going to do?"

"What?" they said.

Mr Gregg looked at them and smiled. "We are going to build a nest."

"A nest!" they said. "Can we do that?"

"We *must* do it," said Mr Gregg. "We've got to have somewhere to sleep. Follow me."

They flew off to a tall tree, and right at the top of it Mr Gregg chose the place for the nest.

"Now we want sticks," he said. "Lots and lots of little sticks. Off you go, all of you, and find them and bring them back here."

"But we have no hands!" said Philip.

"Then use your mouths."

Mrs Gregg and the children flew off. Soon they were

back, carrying sticks in their mouths. Mr Gregg took the sticks and started to build the nest.

"More," he said. "I want more and more and more sticks. Keep going."

The nest began to grow. Mr Gregg was very good at making the sticks stick together.

After a while he said, "That's enough sticks. Now I want leaves and feathers and things like that to make the inside nice and soft."

The building of the nest went on and on. It took a long time. But at last it was finished.

"Try it," said Mr Gregg, hopping back. He was very pleased with his work.

"Oh, isn't it lovely!" cried Mrs Gregg, going into it and sitting down. "I feel I might lay an egg any moment!"

The others all got in beside her.

"How warm it is!" said William.

"And what fun to be living so high up," said Philip. "We may be small, but nobody can hurt us up here."

"But what about food?" said Mrs Gregg. "We haven't had a thing to eat all day."

"That's right," Mr Gregg said, "So we will now fly back to the house and go in by an open window and get the tin of biscuits when the ducks aren't looking."

"Oh, we will be pecked to bits by those dirty great ducks!" cried Mrs Gregg.

"We shall be very careful, my love," said Mr Gregg. And off they went.

But when they got to the house, they found all the windows and doors closed. There was no way in.

"Just look at that beastly duck cooking at my stove!" cried Mrs Gregg as she flew past the kitchen window. "How dare she!"

"And look at that one holding my lovely gun!"

shouted Mr Gregg.

"One of them is lying in my bed!" yelled William,

looking into a top window. "

And one of them is playing with my electric train!" cried Philip.

"Oh, dear! Oh, dear!" said Mrs Gregg. "They have taken over our whole house! We shall never get it back. And what are we going to eat?"

"I will not eat worms," said Philip. "I would rather die."

"Or slugs," said William.

Mrs Gregg took the two boys under her wings and hugged them. "Don't worry," she said. "I can mince it all up very fine and you won't even know the difference. Lovely slugburgers. Delicious wormburgers."

"Oh no!" cried William. "Never!" said Philip.

"Disgusting!" said Mr Gregg. "Just because we have wings, we don't have to eat bird food. We shall eat apples instead. Our trees are full of them. Come on!"

So they flew off to an apple tree.

But to eat an apple without holding it in your hands is not at all easy. Every time you try to get your teeth into it, it just pushes away. In the end, they were able to get a few small bites each. And then it began to get dark, so they all flew back to the nest and lay down to sleep.

It must have been at about this time that I, back in my own house, picked up the telephone and tried to call Philip. I wanted to see if the family was all right.

"Hello," I said.

"Quack!" said a voice at the other end.

"Who is it?" I asked.

"Quack—quack!"

"Philip," I said, "is that you?"

"Quack—quack—quack—quack—quack!"

"Oh, stop it!" I said.

Then there came a very funny noise. It was like a bird laughing.

I put down the telephone quickly.

"Oh, that Magic Finger!" I cried. "What *has* it done to my friends?"

That night, while Mr and Mrs Gregg and Philip and William were trying to get some sleep up in the high nest, a great wind began to blow. The tree rocked from side to side, and everyone, even Mr Gregg, was afraid that the

nest would fall down. Then came the rain. It rained and rained, and the water ran into the nest and they all got as wet as could be—and oh, it was a bad, bad night!

At last the morning came, and with it the warm sun.

"Well!" said Mrs Gregg. "Thank goodness that's over! I never want to sleep in a nest again!" She got up and looked over the side . . .

"Help!" she cried. "Look! Look down there!"

"What is it, my love?" said Mr Gregg. He stood up and peeped over the side.

He got the surprise of his life!

On the ground below them stood the four enormous ducks, as tall as men, and three of them were holding guns in their hands. One had Mr Gregg's gun, one had Philip's gun, and one had William's gun.

The guns were all pointing right up at the nest.

"No! No! No!" called out Mr and Mrs Gregg, both together, "Don't shoot! Please don't shoot!"

"Why not?" said one of the ducks. It was the one who wasn't holding a gun. "You are always shooting at us."

"Oh, but that's not the same!" said Mr Gregg. "We are allowed to shoot ducks!"

"Who allows you?" asked the duck.

"We allow each other," said Mr Gregg.

"Very nice," said the duck. "And now *we* are going to allow each other to shoot you."

(I would have loved to have seen Mr Gregg's face just then.)

"Oh, *please!*" cried Mrs Gregg.

"My two little children are up here with us! You wouldn't shoot *my* children!"

"Yesterday you shot *my* children," said the duck. "You shot all six of my children."

"I'll never do it again!" cried Mr Gregg. "Never, never, never!"

"Do you really mean that?" asked the duck."

"I *do* mean it!" said Mr Gregg. "I'll never shoot another duck as long as I live!"

"That is not good enough," said the duck. "What about deer?"

"I'll do anything you say if you will only put down those guns!" cried Mr Gregg. "I'll never shoot another duck or another deer or anything else again!"

"Will you give me your word on that?" said the duck.

"I will! I will!" said Mr Gregg.

"Will you throw away your guns?" asked the duck.

"I will break them into tiny bits!" said Mr Gregg.

"And never again need you be afraid of me or my family."

"Very well," said the duck. "You may now come down. And by the way, may I congratulate you on the nest. For a first effort it's pretty good."

Mr and Mrs Gregg and Philip and William hopped out of the nest and flew down.

Then all at once everything went black before their

eyes, and they couldn't see. At the same time a funny

feeling came over them all, and they heard a great wind

blowing in their ears.

Then the black that was before their eyes turned to

blue, to green, to red, and then to gold, and suddenly, there they were, standing in lovely bright sunshine in their own

garden, near their own house, and everything was back to

normal once again.

"Our wings have gone!" cried Mr Gregg. "And our arms have come back!"

"And we are not tiny any more!" laughed Mrs Gregg. "Oh, I am so glad!"

Philip and William began dancing about with joy.

Then, high above their heads, they heard the call of a wild duck. They all looked up, and they saw the four birds, lovely against the blue sky, flying very close together, heading back to the lake in the woods.

It must have been about half an hour later that I myself walked into the Greggs'

garden. I had come to see how things were going, and I must admit I was expecting the worst. At the gate I stopped and stared. It was a queer sight.

In one corner Mr Gregg was smashing all three guns

into tiny pieces with a huge hammer.

In another corner Mrs Gregg was placing beautiful flowers upon sixteen tiny mounds of soil which I learned later were the graves of the ducks that had been shot the day before.

And in the middle of the yard stood Philip and William,
with a sack of their father's best barley beside them. They
were surrounded by ducks, doves, pigeons, sparrows,
robins, larks, and many other kinds that I did not know, and
the birds were eating the barley that the boys were scattering
by the handful.

"Good morning, Mr Gregg," I said.

Mr Gregg lowered his hammer and looked at me. "My name is not Gregg any more," he said. "In honour of my feathered friends, I have changed it from Gregg to Egg."

"And I am Mrs Egg," said Mrs Gregg.

"What happened?" I asked. They seemed to have gone completely dotty[11], all four of them.

Philip and William then began to tell me the whole story. When they had finished, William said, "Look! There's the nest! Can you see it? Right up in the top of the tree! That's where we slept last night!"

"I built it *all* myself," Mr Egg said proudly. "Every stick of it."

"If you don't believe us," Mrs Egg said, "just go into the house and take a look at the bathroom. It's a mess."

"They filled the tub right up to the brim," Philip said. "They must have been swimming around in it all night! And feathers everywhere!"

"Ducks like water," Mr Egg said. "I'm glad they had a good time."

Just then, from somewhere over by the lake, there

came a loud BANG!

"Someone's shooting!" I cried.

"That'll be Jim Cooper," Mr Egg said. "Him and his three boys. They're shooting mad, those Coopers are, the whole family."

Suddenly I started to see red . . .

Then I got very hot all over . . .

Then the tip of my finger began tingling most terribly.

I could feel the power building up and up inside me . . .

I turned and started running towards the lake as fast as I could.

"Hey!" shouted Mr Egg. "What's up? Where are you going?"

"To find the Coopers," I called back.

"But Why?"

"You wait and see!" I said. "They'll be nesting in the trees tonight, every one of them!"

查單字

1 go off：離開（而準備進行某種活動……）

2 mind one's p's and q's：謹言慎行；留心舉止；小心翼翼（小孩學習字母時，容易把 p 和 q 混淆，大人會叮囑他們留意二者的的不同。衍伸為「循規蹈矩」之意。）

3 see red：勃然大怒、憤怒。

4 Oh, dear!：天啊！

5 good and …：（後面接形容詞）極，很，非常；為形容詞用法。

6 tingle：感覺刺痛。

7 beside oneself：忘形、忘我；對自己的情緒失控（後面常接 with）。

beside oneself with joy：得意忘形；欣喜若狂。

8 but：原意為「但是」，在這裡是表示「哇！喔！天哪！」驚訝之意。

9 now then：那麼……（用來提醒對方注意，或表示警告、提出抗議）；好了，行了（表示勸阻或寬慰）。

10 it isn't any good：與「no good」和「no use」同義。

11 dotty：古怪的、瘋狂的。

羅爾德・達爾

出生：1916 年於英國威爾斯地德蘭道夫誕生

學歷：雷普敦聖彼得市德蘭道夫天主教學校

職業：殼牌石油公司東非代表。第二次世界大戰英
　　　國皇家空軍戰鬥機飛行員，空軍武官，作家。

　　達爾有一間特別建造的寫作小屋，座落在 Great Missenden 住家的蘋果園旁。他在裡面完成所有的童書寫作。他坐在母親的扶手椅上，還在上頭挖了個凹洞，好減輕背痛的壓力。

　　達爾將故事的所有靈感寫在一本用舊了的紅色練習本裡，而且寫作之前，總要先準備好六枝削尖的鉛筆和一種美式拍紙簿，每日持之以恆的寫作。達爾常將故事的部分情節重新寫過，好讓內容讀起來更有趣、更好看。他還習慣在他的小屋外頭，把那些不要的稿紙生火燒掉呢。

達爾於一九九〇年去世，享年七十四歲。

生活座右銘

我在兩端同時燒著蠟燭

雖然無法明亮終宵。

但是，

啊，我的敵人和朋友們，

它散發出迷人光彩。

你可以到羅爾德 ・ 達爾的網站上尋找更多與他有關的事情：www.roalddahl.com

羅爾德‧達爾
不只說精采的故事……

你知道嗎？本書作者版稅的 10% 會捐給
羅爾德‧達爾慈善機構嗎？

●羅爾達‧達爾優良兒童慈善機構（Roald Dahl's Marvellous Children's Charity）：羅爾德‧達爾以故事和韻文聞名，但鮮為人知的是，他其實常常幫助罹患重症的兒童。所以現在羅爾達‧達爾優良兒童慈善機構秉承他不凡的善行，幫助數以千計罹患神經或血液相關疾病的孩童，以期接近達爾善良的心。此機構也為英國孩童提供護理照料、醫療設備，以及很重要的──娛樂，並透過先驅研究幫助世界各地的孩童。

你願意拿出實際行動來幫助別人嗎？

詳情請看：www.roalddahlcharity.org。

●羅爾德‧達爾博物館暨故事中心（Roald Dahl Museum and Story Centre）：設立於倫敦郊外的白金漢郡大密森頓市，也是羅爾德‧達爾生前居住與寫作的地方。達爾的信件與手稿展示於博物館的中心位置；另外還有兩間展示達爾生平、充滿童趣的展覽室：一間互動式的故事中心，以及他著名的寫作小屋。

羅爾達‧達爾優良兒童慈善機構為正式註冊的慈善團體，登記字號為 1137409。
羅爾德‧達爾博物館暨故事中心為正式註冊的慈善團體，登記字號為 1085853。
羅爾德‧達爾信託基金（The Roald Dahl Charitable Trust）為新成立的慈善機構，以支援上列二個團體的運作。
＊注：版稅捐款已扣除佣金。

國家圖書館出版品預行編目資料

神奇魔指 / 羅爾德‧達爾（Roald Dahl）著；
昆丁‧布雷克（Quentin Blake）繪；顏銘新譯. --
二版 . --台北市：幼獅，2013.09
　面；　公分. --（故事館；10）
譯自：The Magic Finger
ISBN 978-957-574-923-1（平裝）

873.59　　　　　　　　　　102015330

・故事館010・

神奇魔指

作　　　者＝羅爾德‧達爾（Roald Dahl）
繪　　　圖＝昆丁‧布雷克（Quentin Blake）
譯　　　者＝顏銘新
出 版 者＝幼獅文化事業股份有限公司
發 行 人＝葛永光
總 經 理＝王華金
總 編 輯＝林碧琪
主　　　編＝沈怡汝
編　　　輯＝白宜平
美術編輯＝游巧鈴
總 公 司＝10045台北市重慶南路1段66-1號3樓
電　　　話＝(02)2311-2832
傳　　　真＝(02)2311-5368
郵政劃撥＝00033368

印　　　刷＝崇寶彩藝印刷股份有限公司
定　　　價＝180元
港　　　幣＝60元
二　　　版＝2013.09
二　　　刷＝2022.09
書　　　號＝987216

幼獅樂讀網
http://www.youth.com.tw
幼獅購物網
http://shopping.youth.com.tw
e-mail:customer@youth.com.tw

THE MAGIC FINGER by Roald Dahl and illustrated by Quentin Blake
Copyright© Roald Dahl Nominee Ltd.,1966
Complex Chinese translation copyright©2004 by YOUTH CULTURAL ENTERPRISE COMPANY
Published by arrangement with David Higham Associates Ltd.
Through Bardon-Chinese Media Agency
ALL RIGHTS RESERVED

基本資料

姓名： _____ 先生／小姐

婚姻狀況：□已婚 □未婚　職業：□學生 □公教 □上班族 □家管 □其他

出生：民國 _____ 年 _____ 月 _____ 日

電話：（公） _____ （宅） _____ （手機） _____

e-mail： _____

聯絡地址： _____

1.您所購買的書名：　**神奇魔指**

2.您通常以何種方式購書?：□1.書店買書　□2.網路購書　□3.傳真訂購　□4.郵局劃撥
　　（可複選）　　□5.幼獅門市　□6.團體訂購　□7.其他

3.您是否曾買過幼獅其他出版品：□是，□1.圖書　□2.幼獅文藝　□3.幼獅少年
　　　　　　　　　　　　　　　□否

4.您從何處得知本書訊息：□1.師長介紹　□2.朋友介紹　□3.幼獅少年雜誌
　　（可複選）　　□4.幼獅文藝雜誌　□5.報章雜誌書評介紹 _____ 報
　　　　　　　　　□6.DM傳單、海報　□7.書店 □8.廣播(　　　　　　　　)
　　　　　　　　　□9.電子報、edm　□10.其他

5.您喜歡本書的原因：□1.作者　□2.書名　□3.內容　□4.封面設計　□5.其他

6.您不喜歡本書的原因：□1.作者　□2.書名　□3.內容　□4.封面設計　□5.其他

7.您希望得知的出版訊息：□1.青少年讀物　□2.兒童讀物　□3.親子叢書
　　　　　　　　　　　　□4.教師充電系列　□5.其他

8.您覺得本書的價格：□1.偏高　□2.合理　□3.偏低

9.讀完本書後您覺得：□1.很有收穫　□2.有收穫　□3.收穫不多　□4.沒收穫

10.敬請推薦親友，共同加入我們的閱讀計畫，我們將適時寄送相關書訊，以豐富書香與心靈的空間：
(1)姓名 _____ e-mail _____ 電話 _____
(2)姓名 _____ e-mail _____ 電話 _____
(3)姓名 _____ e-mail _____ 電話 _____

11.您對本書或本公司的建議：

10045 台北市重慶南路一段66-1號3樓

幼獅文化事業股份有限公司

客服專線：02-23112832分機208　傳真：02-23115368

e-mail：customer@youth.com.tw

幼獅樂讀網http：//www.youth.com.tw